WOMEN IN THE ARTS

WOMEN IN
Dance

BY PATRICIA HUTCHISON

CONTENT CONSULTANT
Ann Murphy, MFA
Associate Professor
Mills College

Core Library
An Imprint of Abdo Publishing
abdopublishing.com

Cover image: Ballerina Misty Copeland performs at an
awards show called Black Girls Rock in 2013.

abdopublishing.com

Published by Abdo Publishing, a division of ABDO, PO Box 398166, Minneapolis, Minnesota 55439. Copyright © 2019 by Abdo Consulting Group, Inc. International copyrights reserved in all countries. No part of this book may be reproduced in any form without written permission from the publisher. Core Library™ is a trademark and logo of Abdo Publishing.

Printed in the United States of America, North Mankato, Minnesota
042018
092018

Cover Photo: Charles Sykes/Invision/AP images
Interior Photos: Charles Sykes/Invision/AP images, 1, 26; Bebeto Matthews/AP Images, 4–5; Igor Bulgarin/Shutterstock Images, 7 (left); Nigel Norrington/ullstein bild/Getty Images, 7 (middle); Shutterstock Images, 7 (right), 15; Robbie Jack/Corbis Entertainment/Getty Images, 8; Amanda Edwards/Getty Images Entertainment/Getty Images, 10; Album/Fine Arts Images/Newscom, 12–13; Fine Art Images Heritage Images/Newscom, 18; Tom Fitzsimmons/AP Images, 20–21; AP Images, 25, 43; Ron Galella/WireImage/Getty Images, 28–29; Michael Putland/Hulton Archive/Getty Images, 31; Alastair Muir/REX/Shutterstock, 33, 45; Michael Dwyer/AP Images, 34; Mary Altaffer/AP Images Images, 36–37; John Lamparski/Getty Images Entertainment/Getty Images, 39

Editor: Julie Dick
Imprint Designer: Maggie Villaume
Series Design Direction: Claire Vanden Branden

Library of Congress Control Number: 2017962832

Publisher's Cataloging-in-Publication Data

Names: Hutchison, Patricia, author.
Title: Women in dance / by Patricia Hutchison.
Description: Minneapolis, Minnesota : Abdo Publishing, 2019. | Series: Women in the arts | Includes online resources and index.
Identifiers: ISBN 9781532114731 (lib.bdg.) | ISBN 9781532154560 (ebook)
Subjects: LCSH: Women dancers--Juvenile literature. | Women choreographers--Juvenile literature. | Women in the performing arts--Juvenile literature. | Professions--Juvenile literature.
Classification: DDC 792.8--dc23

CONTENTS

CHAPTER
ONE

Misty Copeland

Misty Copeland woke up one morning in 2012 with aching muscles from long hours of dancing. She enjoyed the feeling. That night, she would take the stage in her biggest role yet. The movements she would perform were as familiar as breathing. She glanced in the mirror, imagining the fiery feathered headdress and red glitter on her face. Copeland was the first black woman to play the title role in *The Firebird* for a major ballet company.

That night, Copeland was greeted by the largest crowd she had ever seen. The music started. She could barely hear it over the

Misty Copeland was the first African American woman to be a principal dancer with the American Ballet Theatre (ABT).

thunderous applause. Copeland ran onstage, and the flock of dancers parted. She was the star—she was the Firebird.

There are many types of dance, but they all have some aspects in common. A career in dance requires constant dedication. Dancers sacrifice time with family and friends to perfect their skills. They often find it difficult to balance dance and life outside the studio.

LEARNING TO DANCE

Copeland called herself an "unlikely ballerina" in her book *Life in Motion.* She started ballet lessons at

BALLET COSTUMES

Romantic tutus are knee to ankle length to create an airy look.

Powder puff tutus have a short skirt with no wires.

Pancake tutus are short, with wired frames to keep their shape.

Today's ballet costumes come in different lengths and styles. Some outfits are long and loose. Others are shorter and simpler. Which styles do you see in this chapter? Which type do you think is easiest to dance in?

age 13. Many ballerinas start training in elementary school. Her instructor molded Copeland's body into poses few people could do. She had never seen anyone like Copeland. Her small head, long legs, and big feet made her the perfect ballerina.

Copeland learned quickly. She worked hard and loved dance. She received a standing ovation for her

performance as Claire in *Claire and the Chocolate Nutcracker.* That performance launched Copeland into her career. By age 17, she was dancing with the corps de ballet of the American Ballet Theatre (ABT), one of the best-known ballet programs in the United States.

After a few years, Copeland's body began to change. She grew taller and gained weight. Her confidence began to slip. ABT staff encouraged Copeland to change her eating habits. Copeland gave up unhealthy foods and started eating seafood instead of meat. She didn't want to at first, but she realized it was important to be healthy. After five years, she found her balance. She still had curves. But she knew they were a part of who she was as a dancer.

Copeland's hard work paid off. By the fall of 2011, she had been a soloist for four years. She was studying for the title role in the ballet *The Firebird*. Copeland worked through exhausting classes to learn the difficult choreography. She got the part.

Copeland knew that her story had touched many people's lives. She was afraid she would let them all down. But she didn't need to worry. In June 2015, Copeland was promoted to principal dancer at the ABT. She was the first black woman to reach that status in the history of the company.

STRAIGHT TO THE
SOURCE

In one interview, Copeland explains what she thinks her influence is on ballet:

I think that having a platform and having a voice to be seen by people beyond the classical ballet world has really been my power. . . . I think that being in this position and showing that I can execute and do all of these things that it's possible to have any skin complexion, to have a healthy body image for the ballerina body. I think it's given me more of a voice. And it's I think forcing a lot of these top tier [ballet] companies to address the lack of diversity and diversifying the bodies that we're seeing in classical ballet. It's really forcing that conversation to be had.

Source: Maya Rhodan. "Transcript: President Obama & Misty Copeland in Conversation." *Time*. Time, March 14, 2016. Web. Accessed October 31, 2017.

What's the Big Idea?

Read the quote. What does Copeland say about how her involvement is changing modern ballet? How might ballet corps look different in the future? Give two supporting details from the quote.

A New Era of Dance

The Romantic Movement began in the early 1800s. People wanted to find ways to express themselves naturally. Artists and writers were inspired by nature to create new works. Dancers also began to experiment with new movements.

MARIE TAGLIONI

Marie Taglioni was one of the first ballerinas who danced *en pointe*. Pointe is a ballet technique where a dancer supports all of her weight on the tips of her fully extended feet. To dance en pointe, Taglioni wore regular

Marie Taglioni was one of the first ballerinas to dance en pointe.

ballet slippers with extra stitching at the sides and tops. Today, ballerinas wear pointe shoes with molded support for their toes and the sides of their feet and a flat platform at the end.

Taglioni was born in Sweden in 1804 with a curved spine. Her father, Filippo, wanted her to be a dancer like him despite her curvature. After years of training, her father arranged Taglioni's debut in Vienna, Austria, in January 1822.

Her mother didn't think Taglioni was ready and asked her teacher for his opinion. Her teacher, Jean-François Coulon, claimed she could never be a dancer because of her curved spine. But Taglioni's father gave her private lessons. She worked tirelessly for more than a year, and the Vienna debut was a success. Five years later, Taglioni took the stage at the famous Paris Opera.

Taglioni's performance in *La Sylphide* in 1832 made her famous. Filippo choreographed the ballet especially

POINTE SHOES

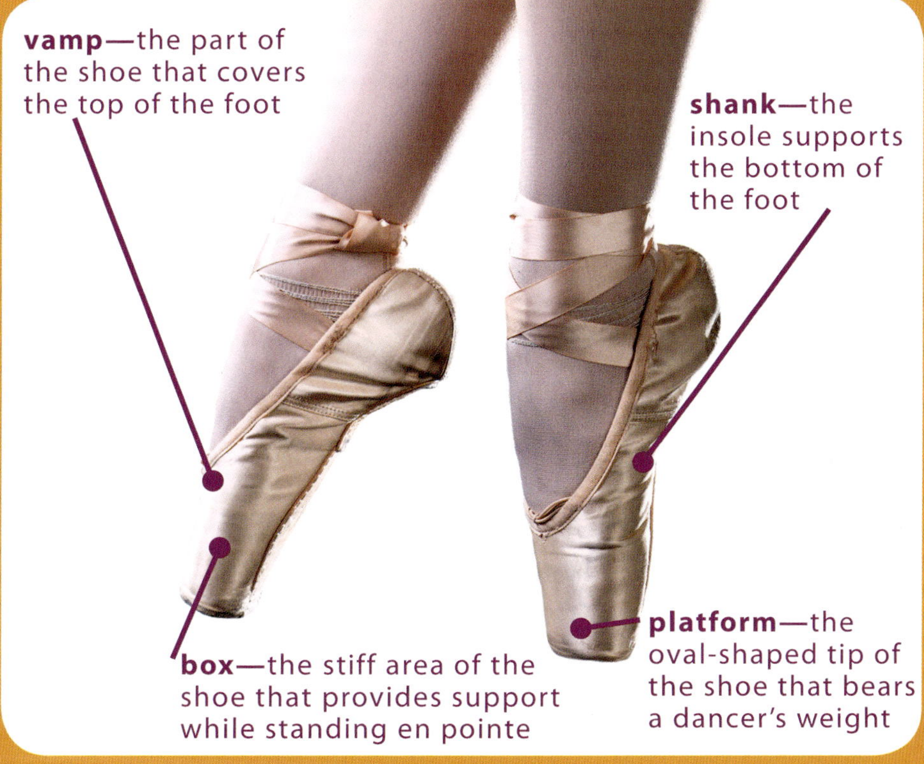

Pointe shoes are designed to support a ballerina's feet. How are they different from shoes you wear?

for his daughter. He created specific poses to hide Taglioni's curved spine. Posing as the fairy, Taglioni's shoulders tilted forward. Her arms rounded gracefully in front of her.

She performed almost the entire ballet on the tips of her toes. Her costume was also a break from tradition. Taglioni was the first ballerina to wear a tutu. The tight top flowed into a fluffy, bell-shaped skirt. It came to the middle of her calves, showing off her delicate footwork.

With her performance, Taglioni started a new genre called "Romantic ballet." Other choreographers began to compose Romantic ballets. Thanks to the new pointe shoe, dancers began to move with greater speed and lightness. They could perform as ghosts or fairies and make soft movements with rounded arms, as Taglioni did in *La Sylphide*.

A choreographer is someone who arranges the steps and movements for a dance. Choreographers work with many levels of dancers. They can create silent dances or routines that flow with the music. They can create it alone or they can ask dancers to invent dance material together. Once the dance is created, the choreographer typically teaches the steps to the performers. In rehearsals, performers practice the movements and timing.

Her costume became known as the Romantic tutu. These costumes and techniques are still widely used.

Meanwhile, in the late 1800s, a new wave of dancers began to experiment with different techniques. This gave rise to "the new dance"—what is called modern dance. Although it used some of the same movements as ballet, modern dancing was more relaxed and free. Instead of telling stories, these expressive dances shared ideas and emotions.

LOIE FULLER

Loie Fuller had no formal training, but

Freestyle Dancing

Most dancers learn basic techniques made of set exercises for the legs, torso, arms, and head. They repeat the movements until they can perform them perfectly. The dances they perform are often made up of the steps of the technique. Today, freestyling is part of many modern dancers' training. They simply put on music and dance. Moving their bodies, they freely express the feelings the music stirs within them.

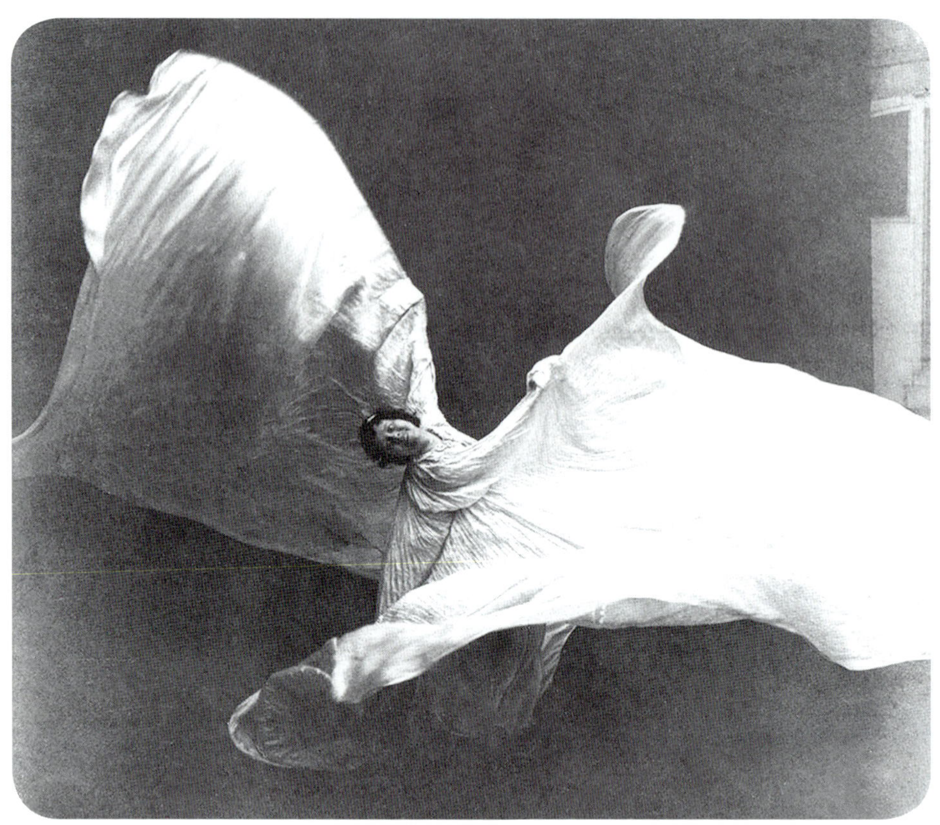

she had some knowledge of the Delsarte movement. Delsarte style emphasized connecting emotions to specific movements. Loie Fuller did this by using simple movements, new kinds of stage lighting, and unexpected music. Fuller spun while waving long, flowing silk through the air. As she moved, colored lights shone on her flowing dress.

Fuller's most famous work was her serpentine dance in Paris during the 1890s. She danced alone, often mimicking natural elements such as a butterfly or fire.

Fuller was the first dancer to insist that the theater be dark during her performance. This enhanced the colored lighting effects that she created. She experimented to create different effects. Later in her life, she became a teacher. She instructed girls in natural movement and creativity. Fuller paved the way for the development of modern dance.

Explore Online

This chapter explores how Marie Taglioni changed ballet. The article at the website below summarizes the history of ballet. What information did you already know? What information was new to you?

The History of Ballet

abdocorelibrary.com/women-in-dance

Dance Pioneers

Dance has continued to change over the years. Some women created new techniques and new styles of dancing. Other women have taught dance, designed costumes, or used dance to help empower girls and women.

MARTHA GRAHAM

Martha Graham is sometimes called the mother of modern dance. She began studying dance in the mid-1910s. She studied at the Denishawn School in California. The school experimented with several different techniques. Some of these imitated Indian or Indonesian styles.

Martha Graham experimented with several dance techniques.

Graham built on those techniques to create her own style. The movements did not have to be fluid. She wanted them to be tense with emotion. Graham's modern dance was not concerned with flow and grace.

The movements were more raw and real. Audiences were not used to this. At first, some critics called her dances ugly.

Many of Graham's dances focus on women and their struggles. Her 1955 dance *Seraphic Dialogue* tells the story of Joan of Arc. She not only choreographed the dance, but she also performed in it.

Isadora Duncan

Isadora Duncan is sometimes called the inventor of modern dance. After several years of ballet lessons, Duncan quit at the age of nine. Practicing the same movements over and over made her feel like a puppet. In the early 1900s, she began to develop her own style of dance. She performed barefoot, wearing flowing costumes and a loose hairstyle. Her free-spirited choreography was an expression of her feelings. Her movements were shocking and inspiring at the same time. Duncan elevated modern dance to an art form.

Another one of her famous works is *Appalachian Spring*. It tells the story of a newly married couple on the American frontier.

CHITA RIVERA

When she was a child, Chita Rivera bounced around her living room. When she broke the coffee table, her mother took her to ballet classes. She knew her daughter needed an outlet for her energy. In 1944, Rivera took her first dance lessons.

Rivera's teacher, Doris Jones, opened the Jones-Haywood School in 1941 in Washington, DC. It was the first ballet school in the United States for children of color. In addition to ballet, Jones taught Rivera about pride, focus, and hard work.

Jones's lessons were demanding. Word about her training style spread to the New York City Ballet. A talent scout asked Rivera to audition for the company. The day of her tryout, Rivera's heart sank. When she got off the elevator, she saw how tall and thin the girls were.

She turned to her teacher, wondering why they had asked a short girl from Puerto Rico to audition. Jones told Rivera to just do what she had taught her to do. Rivera earned a part that day.

Later, she was asked to join the chorus in the musical *Call Me Madam*. Rivera had doubts about taking the job. She wanted to be a ballerina. But she decided to give musical theater a try. Her performance led to another role in *Can Can*. By then, she was hooked on theatrical dancing. Rivera became a famous Broadway dancer.

Contemporary dance is a combination of many dance elements. It is a blend of ballet, modern dance, jazz, international dances, hip-hop, and many more. Some contemporary choreography tells a story based on the music. Other pieces have no story lines. They show the dancer's emotions through movement.

Chita Rivera, *left*, played Anita in the debut of the Broadway musical *West Side Story*.

Rivera performed at the 2015 Tony Awards. The Tonys are given to outstanding theater productions.

In 1957, she starred as Anita in the stage debut of the award-winning musical *West Side Story*. It was the beginning of a long, successful career.

Jones's lessons about life served Rivera well. Jones taught Rivera to never give up. Even when Rivera was hurt in a car accident, she worked hard to get better.

Rivera danced onstage into her 80s. She has been a hit all over the world, including in New York; London, England; and Tokyo, Japan. She has won two Tony Awards. In 2002, Rivera was the first Latina to earn a Kennedy Center Honor. Seven years later, she visited the White House to receive the Presidential Medal of Freedom from President Barack Obama.

Further Evidence

Chita Rivera starred in the debut of the musical *West Side Story*. Read the article about this show at the website below. How has *West Side Story* changed the world of dance? Find a quote from the article that supports your answer.

About West Side Story

abdocorelibrary.com/women-in-dance

Many Roles

ost dancers study movement from a young age. Dance steps become second nature to them. It is only natural that many dancers chose careers in teaching and choreography.

DEBBIE ALLEN

Debbie Allen grew up in Texas during the 1950s and 1960s. The Houston Ballet Foundation (HBF) rejected her when she was 12. At the time, some people didn't think African Americans had the right type of body for ballet. Allen kept trying and was accepted the following year after an instructor saw her dance. She credits HBF's challenging program for pushing her to stardom.

Debbie Allen's fame on the stage led to a career in television.

Broadway dance, often in the form of musicals, combines ballet, jazz, hip-hop, and modern dance with acting and singing. Dance is an important part of the plot. Performers use props such as canes, hats, and gloves. Broadway is a theater district in New York City. But that's not the only place musicals are performed. Professional companies and schools host performances of famous musicals. Some musicals are even adapted into movies.

Allen began her professional career in the Broadway revival of *West Side Story* in 1980. She starred as Anita. Her performance earned her a Tony Award nomination.

Allen also had a small role in the 1980 movie *Fame*. The movie follows high school students as they try to become actors and dancers. In 1982, the movie was adapted into a television series. Allen played demanding dance teacher Lydia Grant. The show ran from 1982 to 1987 and was nominated for several awards. Allen won the 1982 Golden Globe Award for Best Actress in a Musical or Comedy Series.

Soon, her success as a dancer and actress opened other doors. She began directing episodes of *Fame*. She was the first black woman hired as a network television director. After the show was canceled, Allen went on to write, produce, direct, and choreograph the *Debbie Allen Special*. She received two Emmy nominations for this TV variety show.

Allen believes there can be no jazz or modern dance without ballet. In her mind, ballet is the most important foundation for any kind of dance. She says dancers must also have endurance. In *Fame*, Grant tells her students that if they want fame, they must pay for it in sweat. Allen still believes in this advice.

TWYLA THARP

In 1976, Twyla Tharp choreographed *Push Comes to Shove.*

She created it for Mikhail Baryshnikov, a famous Russian ballet dancer. Critics called the performance "groundbreaking." Tharp dressed Baryshnikov in a bowler hat and copper-colored costume. He was part clown, part classical ballet dancer. Since then, Tharp has been in demand throughout the world.

Tharp's dances merge ballet techniques with natural movements. Performers transition from pointe to running and skipping. Tharp combines different forms of movement, such as jazz, ballet, and boxing. Her dancers

perform with technical precision and a casual attitude. Tharp's contemporary choreography erases the divisions between modern dance and classical ballet.

The most unusual parts of Tharp's dances are the endings. All the performers come onstage. They perform different types of dance at the same time. In *Push Comes to Shove*, humor comes together with classical ballet dancers. Russians and Americans dance side by side. These endings express an acceptance of all types of people. Dancers are thrown together onstage and end up performing in perfect harmony.

During the 1960s, ballets were almost exclusively made by men. Tharp had to fight for recognition. She worked hard physically. She believed the only way she would truly know a movement was to perform it herself. Throughout her career, Tharp has choreographed more than 160 works. She has received numerous awards, including a Tony and two Emmys. In 2004, President George W. Bush presented Tharp with the National Medal of Arts. This is the highest award given to artists by the US government.

STRAIGHT TO THE
SOURCE

In an interview in *Harvard Business Review*, Tharp gives her thoughts about failure:

True failure is a mark of accomplishment in the sense that something new and different was tried. Ideally, the best way to fail is in private. In my office, the ratio of failure to success on the dances I create is probably something like six to one. I create about six times more material for my dances than I end up using in the final piece. But I need that unused material to get my one success. I have also sometimes failed in public, and that's very painful. But failing, even in this way, is not useless. It can force you to get yourself together and to produce something new.

Source: Diane Coutu. "Creativity Step by Step." Harvard Business Review. Harvard University, July 31, 2014. Web. Accessed October 16, 2017.

Consider Your Audience

Tharp shows failure in a positive light. How does she think failure helps to create success? Pretend a friend of yours is experiencing failure. Write a note sharing Tharp's advice in your own words. What personal examples could you use?

Expressing Emotions

Dancers create movement with their bodies and their minds. Feelings flow onto the dance floor like paint flows onto an artist's canvas. Some dancers use techniques they were taught. Others create their own.

BLAKELEY WHITE-MCGUIRE

Blakeley White-McGuire started her dance career performing at balls in southern Louisiana. For her first paid performance, she received a crystal bowl instead of money. In 1996, she completed training at the Martha Graham School. Six years later, she was a principal dancer.

In 2009, White-McGuire opened the Paris, France, season dancing in *Errand into the Maze*. This is Graham's dance about conquering fear. Graham described her dance method as a way to explore thoughts and feelings. This is what White-McGuire does when she dances. The roles she performs relate to her life and the lives of her audience. Graham's techniques have helped White-McGuire to perfect her technical skills. They have also helped her to grow as

Promoting Dance

Kayla Collymore is an up-and-coming dancer from New Jersey. She was listed in *Dance Magazine*'s "Top 25 to Watch in 2017." Promoting her craft is an important goal for Collymore. She passes on her knowledge of movement while teaching dance to young children. Through social media, Collymore shares articles, videos, and photos about dance. She also announces upcoming auditions and performances.

an artist. White-McGuire has the confidence to try new movements beyond her skill set. This has brought her unique opportunities in the world of dance.

White-McGuire has performed in many famous productions, including Graham's *Appalachian Spring* and *Chronicle*. She has danced on famous stages all over the world. White-McGuire has earned major honors, including an Italian Career Achievement Award in 2006. When she is not performing, White-McGuire teaches Graham's methods to her own students.

YIN YUE

Yin Yue took her first dance class in Shanghai, China, at the age of four. In 2005, she ranked in the top ten performers in the National Dance Competition. However, she was told that she would never be a professional dancer in China. They said she was too small.

So Yin moved to New York City. There, she earned a master's degree in contemporary dance at New York University in 2008. Although Chinese dance is not dedicated to the individual artist's experience, Yin believes in self expression. She is fast and powerful. She dances to show the way she feels inside.

Yin quickly gained attention as a talented performer

and choreographer. She created her own contemporary dance technique called FoCo. The movements combine Tibetan folk dances with powerful athletics. The choreography is set to chilling music. Quick, sharp gestures combine with fluid body movements. Her personal style is a balance of grace and physical power.

The main themes of Yin's work are emotional experiences and conflicts. These themes are shown in her work *We Have Been Here Before*. The movements in the piece express the idea of past and present. There is no scripted story. Instead, the audience is invited to feel and imagine memories of their own lives. Yin's contemporary work has won several dance competitions.

Women have been a part of dance throughout history. Styles and costumes change over time, but some things stay the same. Dancers dedicate themselves to their art, work hard, and develop their skills.

NOTABLE
WORKS

The Firebird

The Firebird, by Russian composer Igor Stravinsky, was originally performed in Paris in 1910. A magical firebird helps a prince fight an evil enchanter to rescue a princess.

La Sylphide

La Sylphide, by Filippo Taglioni, was first performed in 1832 and marks the debut of pointe dance in ballet. A winged spirit, called a sylph, wakes a young man on the day of his wedding. He falls in love with her and tries to win her love.

Appalachian Spring

Appalachian Spring by Martha Graham opened in 1944. It tells the story of a young pioneer couple at the beginning of their life together.

West Side Story

West Side Story tells the story of two rival gangs in 1950s New York City. The sister of one of the gang leaders falls in love with someone from the other gang, leading to tragedy. The story is similar to Shakespeare's play *Romeo and Juliet*.

STOP AND THINK

Surprise Me

Many of the stars mentioned in this book faced enormous difficulties before they became famous dancers. Which star's struggle surprised you the most? Write down two hardships she had to overcome before she could realize her dreams. Write a few sentences about each one. Why did you find these struggles most surprising?

Take a Stand

This book tells about the sacrifices dancers must make for their careers. Do you think the rewards are worth the sacrifices that they make? Explain why you feel this way.

You Are There

Choose your favorite style of dance presented in this book. Imagine you have met one of the stars mentioned for that type of dance. What questions would you ask?

Another View

The author of this book said Martha Graham is sometimes called the mother of modern dance. Ask an adult to help you find another source about the beginning of modern dance. Write a short essay comparing and contrasting the new source with this book. What is the point of view of each author? How are they similar and why? How are they different and why?

GLOSSARY

choreography
the steps and movements
planned for a dance

debut
the first public performance
of a dancer or a production

enhanced
added to the strength or
beauty of something

ensemble
a group of performers who
act together

influence
having an effect on someone
or something

inspiration
a person, place, or
experience that gives
someone an idea to do or
create something

pointe
a ballet position where the
dancer raises herself up
on tiptoe

productions
performances of dances

promoted
moved to a higher position
or rank

technique
how a dancer uses
basic movements

tradition
a way of doing something
that a group has used for a
long time

ONLINE RESOURCES

To learn more about women in dance, visit our free resource websites below.

Visit **abdocorelibrary.com** for free Common Core resources for teachers and students, including vetted activities, multimedia, and booklinks, for deeper subject comprehension.

Visit **abdobooklinks.com** for free additional online weblinks for further learning. These links are routinely monitored and updated to provide the most current information available.

LEARN MORE

Copeland, Misty. *Life in Motion: An Unlikely Ballerina*. Young Readers edition. New York: Aladdin Books, 2016.

Hackett, Jane. *How to—Ballet: A Step-by-Step Guide to the Secrets of Ballet*. New York: DK, 2011.

INDEX

About the Author

Patricia Hutchison was a classroom teacher for many years. Now she teaches through her writing. She loves researching and writing about people, science, and history. When she is not writing, Patricia likes to travel with her family to explore new places.